CLUELESS MCGEE

Jeff Mack

PHILOMEL BOOKS
An Imprint of Penguin Group (USA) Inc.

FOR DILLON

PHILOMEL BOOKS

A division of Penguin Young Readers Group. Published by The Penguin Group.

Penguin Group (USA) Inc., 375 Hudson Street, New York, NY 10014, U.S.A.

Penguin Group (Canada), 90 Eglinton Avenue East, Suite 700, Toronto,
Ontario M4P 2Y3, Canada (a division of Pearson Penguin Canada Inc.).

Penguin Books Ltd, 80 Strand, London WC2R ORL, England.

Penguin Ireland, 25 St. Stephen's Green, Dublin 2, Ireland
(a division of Penguin Books Ltd).

Penguin Group (Australia), 250 Camberwell Road, Camberwell, Victoria 3124, Australia
(a division of Pearson Australia Group Pty Ltd).

Penguin Books India Pvt Ltd, 11 Community Centre, Panchsheel Park,
New Delhi—110 017, India.

Penguin Group (NZ), 67 Apollo Drive, Rosedale, Auckland 0632, New Zealand
(a division of Pearson New Zealand Ltd).

Penguin Books (South Africa) (Pty) Ltd, 24 Sturdee Avenue, Rosebank,
Johannesburg 2196, South Africa.

Penguin Books Ltd, Registered Offices: 80 Strand, London WC2R ORL, England.

Published simultaneously in Canada. Printed in the United States of America.

Edited by Michael Green. Design by Semadar Megged.
The illustrations are rendered in pencil on paper.

Library of Congress Cataloging-in-Publication Data
Mack, Jeff. Clueless McGee / Jeff Mack. p. cm. Summary: Through a series of
letters to his father, a private investigator, fifth-grader PJ "Clueless" McGee tells of his
efforts to discover who stole macaroni and cheese from the school cafeteria.
[1. Behavior—Fiction. 2. Schools—Fiction. 3. Private investigators—Fiction. 4. Robbers and
outlaws—Fiction. 5. Letters. 6. Humorous stories.] I. Title. PZ7.M18973Clu 2012
[Fic]—dc23 2012000425
978-0-399-25749-0

10 9 8 7 6 5 4 3 2 1

CHAPTER ONE
THE NINJA SUIT LETTER

SUNDAY, MARCH 31

Dear Dad,

It's me, PJ! How come you moved? Did the bad guys find your secret hideout again?

This week your postcard came from North Dakota. Is that any closer to where me and Mom and Chloe live?

Ever since you told me about the SECRET MISSION, I've been thinking about becoming a private eye like you. That way we could fight bad guys together!

Most kids in 5th grade say they're going to be rock stars or professional basketball players when they grow up. But those are just crazy dreams. We both know it's a lot more realistic if I just follow in your footsteps.

Plus, I already made my own business card.

Check this out:

Pretty awesome, huh? Can I come out to North Dakota and help you with the SECRET MISSION?

I'm already a master of self-defense. I just started playing this awesome video game called NINJA WARZ, and I've learned some incredible moves:

THE SAMURAI SLIDE!

POW!

THE TIGER TACKLE!

POW!
POW!
POW!

POW! THE FALCON FLIP!

POW!

Mom says my moves are getting too dangerous to practice indoors, so you can tell I'm AWESOME!

I just hope I get to use them on some real bad guys soon. She gets mad at me when I practice on Chloe's stuffed animals.

Here are some other reasons I should be your partner:

1. I'm incredibly smart. Especially for 5th grade. Mrs. Sikes says I'm already reading books meant for 6th-graders.

MY
BRAIN:
5 TIMES
AS BIG
AS A
NORMAL
BRAIN!!
← NORMAL
BRAIN!!

FEEL THE POWER!!

2. I'm incredibly brave. Me and Chloe watched Zombie Food Fight on TV five times already. Chloe's only six, so she cried a lot. But I wasn't scared once. I swear!

3. I'm incredibly fast. Whenever a bad guy tries to steal my lunch, I can ALWAYS outrun him.

4. I'm a man who can keep a secret. Got a SECRET MISSION for me? (Hint! Hint!) I won't tell a soul. Not even for a trillion dollars.

And most important . . .

5. I have the SECRET PAJAMAS that you sent me. I know the box said TOP SECRET, but Mom saw me opening it, so I had to tell her. I hope that's OK.

Oh, yeah. I told Chloe too. Sorry about that.

Here's a picture of me wearing the pajamas:

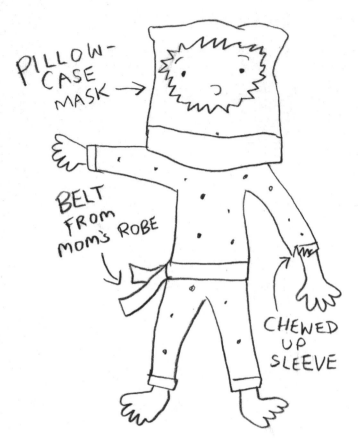

PILLOW-
CASE
MASK →

BELT
FROM
mom's ROBE

CHEWED
UP
SLEEVE

All I did was add a belt and a mask, and they automatically became the perfect ninja suit!

Cool, huh? As you can see, the mask is really just a pillowcase. Only, I had to cut a hole in it so I could see. Don't tell Mom, OK?

You also may have noticed that the sleeve is kind of chewed up. Mom keeps bugging me about that. I've told her over and over that I'll quit chewing, but I guess promising something TEN TIMES just isn't enough for her.

She says if I end up ruining them, she's going to throw them in the

TRASH!

Think about it, Dad!

That makes NO sense!

I mean, if she's so worried about me ruining them, then why does she want to throw them away? Anyway, I think I solved the problem: GUM!

LITTLE BOY BLEW

SUGAR FREE BUBBLE GUM

From now on, when I get ready for bed, I'll just chew some sugar-free gum. If I keep my teeth busy, they won't be able to chew on my sleeve. I tried it out last night, and it worked!

There was just one problem. Somehow a big blob of it got stuck to the pillow while I was sleeping. When  I lifted my head, the whole pillow came up with it.

You might think I'd be mad about having a pillow stuck to my head with sugar-free gum, but I like to look on the bright side of things:

If it wasn't for the pillow, I could have gone all day with gum in my hair and never even noticed!

How lucky is that!

Mom had to cut a lot of my hair to get the pillow off. She seemed kind of mad about it, but I told her to look on the bright side with me:

It didn't help. The gum must have stuck to her scissors, because the more she cut, the madder she got. By the end, the gum was gone, but her scissors were pretty much ruined!

Still, I don't see why she's so mad. I'm the one who has to live with this ugly bald spot.

I look like a zombie!

See? Even Chloe thinks so:

Luckily, I found your old trucker hat in the attic. I told Mom I'll just have to wear it to school every day until my hair grows back.

Mom says it would be rude to wear such a foolish-looking hat to school. I think it would look more foolish to be bald, but she doesn't agree.

Just between me and you, my principal is pretty much the biggest frog-smacker in the whole school. Everyone thinks he looks foolish.

MR. PRINCE
(OUR PRINCIPAL)

SHINY BALD HEAD →

CHEESY BROWN MUSTACHE

BULL HORN FOR YELLING AT KIDS ↓

CHEESY PURPLE SUIT

PANTS TOO HIGH OR TOO SHORT?

As you know, I could argue with Mom for twenty hours straight, but it wouldn't do any good.

So my new plan is to hide the hat in my backpack and wear it when I get on the bus tomorrow. As a fellow private eye, you have to admit this is pretty sneaky!

Well, I'd better get back to practicing my ninja moves. I want to be ready for my new job.

Write back soon, OK?

If I'm going to be your partner, I need to know EVERYTHING about the SECRET MISSION!

Love,

PJ

CHAPTER TWO
THE MAC AND CHEESE LETTER

MONDAY, APRIL 1

Dear Dad,

Well, the hat trick didn't work. As soon as I walked into class, Mrs. Sikes made me take it off. I guess she wanted everyone to stare at MY bald spot all day instead of staring at HERS.

I tried covering the spot with my arm so that no one would notice me. But she had a problem with that too.

Even worse, the ceiling was leaking. So during silent reading time, a big drop of water landed right on my bald spot. It was so loud, everyone in class heard it.

One thing I've learned at this school: if you want to get out of something embarrassing, you have to turn it into something funny. So I sprang into action with a joke . . .

. . . but no one laughed.

Another thing I've learned: a lot of people at this school have no sense of humor.

Mrs. Sikes told me if I didn't like getting dripped on, I should change desks.

The only free desk was the tiny kindergarten desk next to hers that she calls "the Hot Spot." Usually it's just for troublemakers, but for some reason, she made me sit there. Everyone laughed at THAT.

It figures.

On the bright side, there were only twenty minutes until lunch. The menu said we were having mac and cheese today! So I spent the whole time thinking about that.

Our lunch lady, Mrs. Browny, makes amazing mac and cheese. Some kids say if you eat enough of it, you can get super cheese power! But you have to be careful. I once ate so much I almost exploded! So now I just do it for the awesome taste.

Last year, my 4th-grade teacher, Mr. Randall, made everyone write love poems. So I wrote mine about Mrs. Browny's mac and cheese.

Back then, I was seriously thinking about becoming a rock star. So you can imagine this poem as the lyrics to an awesome hit single! Just listen:

SUPER CHEESE POWER!
A LOVE SONG   BY PJ McGEE

MRS. BROWNY MAKES THE BEST!
HER MAC AND CHEESE IS TRULY BLESSED.
EAT A GALLON! BE MY GUEST.
IN THE NUDE OR FULLY DRESSED,

IN THE BATH OR IN THE SHOWER,
IT IS SWEET AND NEVER SOUR.
I COULD EAT IT TWICE AN HOUR
JUST TO FEEL ITS CHEESY POWER!

THE MORE YOU EAT, THE MORE YOU CHEW.
IT ALSO MAKES A SUPER GLUE
THAT YOU CAN USE TO FIX YOUR SHOE
IF THAT IS WHAT YOU WANT TO DO.

OH, MAC AND CHEESE,
    I **LOVE** YOU!! ♡ ♡
♡   ♡   ♡   ♡   ♡

Well, that's it! What do you think? It's pretty much my best poem ever.

Mr. Randall said that you can't really be in love with your lunch, but we both know that's not true. Pretty much everyone here is in love with Mrs. Browny's mac and cheese.

Well, everyone except for the kids at the cheese-allergy table.

So imagine my shock and horror when I got
to lunch and found out the mac and cheese was
STOLEN!

The cafeteria looked like a total crime scene.
Mr. Toots, the janitor, was setting up orange
caution cones in the lunch line.

Mrs. Browny was crying her head off.

Plus, a lot of kids were starting to freak out!

As usual, Mrs. Sikes tried to calm everyone down . . .

. . . but it was no use.

These kids were mad. They wanted their mac and cheese, and they wanted it now!

That's when Mr. Prince walked in. You could tell he was really mad because he was carrying his bullhorn.

Whenever Mr. Prince gets mad, he makes these loud announcements. Only, they're so loud, you can't even understand what he's yelling about.

This time, his bullhorn didn't work. Instead, it just made this weird buzzing noise. That only made him madder.

He shook it. He banged it. He held it up and looked inside.

WHAT ON EARTH?

A big blob of mac and cheese fell out right onto his face.

SPLAT!

Mrs. Browny screamed in terror!

Mr. Prince was furious.

Luckily, I have an incredible eye for detail. Otherwise he never would have seen the tiny piece of paper that was stuck to his forehead.

I took a closer look.

It said:

Watch out, frog-smackers!
There's more where this came from.
Love,
The Mac and Cheese Bandit

Everyone gasped! It was a CLUE!

I had to act fast!

I tried to grab the note, but Mr. Prince
wouldn't let me.

Can you believe it, Dad? This is a job for a
real private eye! I'll bet none of these adults
have ever solved a crime in their life.

I handed Mr. Prince my new business card. Then I walked away. All I can say is it's a good thing I was there to help. Without me, things would have been a total mess.

When we got home, Chloe tried to tell Mom what happened. Except she got the story completely wrong! First she said that Mrs. Browny LOST the mac and cheese.

Then she told Mom that I kept interrupting everyone and getting in the way.

I know she's only six, but she should really check her facts before she starts spreading these lies!

I tried to explain what REALLY happened to the mac and cheese, but Mom just told me to go read quietly by myself.

So I guess she doesn't care about the truth either!

CHEW
CHEW
CHEW

I have to admit I'm a little nervous about this case. I'm the only private eye in the whole school. So everyone is counting on ME to catch the Mac and Cheese Bandit. I only hope I can do it before he strikes again.

All I know is when I do, it will be the greatest day of my entire life!

Love,

PJ

CHAPTER THREE
THE FOOD FIGHT LETTER

TUESDAY, APRIL 2

Dear Dad,

Today was the worst day of my entire life.

It all started with band practice.

Band is probably my least favorite subject, right after math, science, social studies, English, Chinese, and gym.

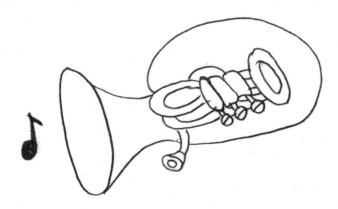

I mostly blame my band teacher, Mr. Pastrami. This is only a drawing of him, but it's EXACTLY what he looks like:

MR. PASTRAMI

Did you notice all of the sweat? That's because he gets really excited when he conducts.

It's not a big deal. Except when he waves his
arms around. Then the sweat goes flying onto US!

Mr. Pastrami is insanely in love with this weird
old music called jazz. He even has a framed
poster of his hero,
"Tuba Cheeks"
Jackson, hanging in
the band room.

TUBA CHEEKS

Plus, Mr. Pastrami plays the tuba during every single one of our concerts. Partly because he's the only one strong enough to lift it. But mostly because it's his big chance to do a solo.

He gets so excited, he plays NONSTOP for twenty or thirty minutes! Pretty much everyone falls asleep after the first minute, but he doesn't even notice.

I signed up to play the drums this year. But it turned out there were already twelve drummers in band and only three drum kits. So I have to play the cymbals.

It was either that or the triangle. And anything is more fun than playing the triangle.

At first I thought playing the cymbals would be cool. But it turns out I only get to smash them once or twice at the end of each song. The rest of the time, I just stand there and watch everyone else play.

On the bright side, I just realized that the cymbals look exactly like the Samurai Shields from NINJA WARZ. So now I can practice my moves while I'm waiting to smash them.

Plus, they protect me from all of Mr. Pastrami's flying sweat!

There's only one problem . . .

They don't protect me from getting yelled at when I drop them.

The real reason today was so terrible is because of a kid in band named Jack B.

JACK B.

EVIL-LOOKING EYEBROWS →

SPIKY HAIR

CHEWS BARBECUE FLAVORED BUBBLE GUM

DIRT SPOTS →

HOLES IN PANTS →

WEARS THE SAME SKULL SHIRT EVERY SINGLE DAY

Jack is also the only 5th-grader with a mustache. It's kind of hard to see, but if you look close, it's right above his lip.

Jack plays the trombone, but he mostly spends band practice picking on Max Orobo.

MAX

Max is the only boy in school who plays the clarinet. For some reason, that makes him the perfect target for bullies.

Jack is always bumping Max's chair with his trombone like it's an accident. But you can tell it's not really.

Today when we were putting the instruments away, Jack stole Max's clarinet.

Then he stuck his barbecue gum on it and threw it to me!

There was no way I was going to get yelled at for that too. Or get Jack's gum on my hands.

So I did the smart thing and pretended not to see it.

It didn't work. Mr. Pastrami came out and yelled at all three of us.

I guess he believed me, since he only sent Max and Jack to the office.

TUBA CHEEKS

I'LL GET YOU FOR THIS, CLUELESS!

I have to say, I felt a little bad for Max. I don't really think he should have gotten in trouble.

Even if he is kind of a frog-smacker.

Later, at lunch, the mac and cheese was still missing. So Mrs. Browny served some gross baked beans instead.

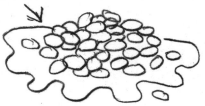

You could tell everyone was really sad about it.

Everyone except for the kids at the cheese-allergy table.

Since none of the adults were doing anything to catch the Mac and Cheese Bandit, I decided to hang up this poster:

Then I went and sat next to Dante Donahue.

Dante is only in 3rd grade, but I let him hang out with me sometimes so I can practice ninja moves on him.

I feel sort of bad for Dante. He doesn't have a lot of crime-fighting skills like me. Maybe because he's still just a little kid.

I guess you could say his most valuable skill is being able to eat gross stuff. For example, he once made fifty cents by eating a Tater Tot after Taylor Wong licked it!

Anyway, me and Dante were trying to figure out the Mac and Cheese Bandit's secret identity when guess who came over to our table?

Jack dumped his backpack onto the table. It was filled with mac and cheese!

Did this mean Jack was the bandit? Was he really turning himself in?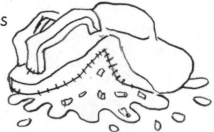

I figured if I played it cool, he might lead me to where the rest of the mac and cheese was hidden!

Good thing I'm naturally cool under pressure.

Too bad Dante isn't.

Jack grabbed a handful of mac and cheese and smooshed it right on my bald spot.

I tried to figure out how to turn it into a joke. But somehow I ended up throwing the whole backpack at him. He ducked right as Dante came back with Mr. Prince. Just my luck!

I tried to tell Mr. Prince that I was innocent, but for some reason, he wouldn't believe me.

He didn't even believe me when I told him Jack was probably the bandit. He just sent me to his office.

Half an hour later, he came in wearing a T-shirt and jeans. I have to say, he didn't look very principally carrying his cheesy suit around in a plastic bag.

CAN YOU BELIEVE IT, DAD? ME? A TROUBLEMAKER? I'd hardly call solving crimes and catching bandits being a troublemaker.

Mr. Prince was acting like the whole thing was MY fault.

I could only think of one thing:

Mr. Prince shook his head and handed me the bag.

Clean his suit? With ninja moves? How am I supposed to do that? Especially without Mom finding out?

What have I done, Dad? That mac and cheese was my only clue. And I threw it away!

Now I'm clueless.

I'll bet I wouldn't have all this trouble if I was living with you in North Dakota.

Love,

PJ

PS. Another reason this was the worst day ever: guess what Mom made for dinner tonight.

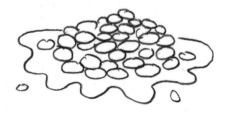

It figures.

CHAPTER FOUR
THE WET PANTS LETTER

WEDNESDAY, APRIL 3

Dear Dad,

Check it out! I found the perfect place to hide Mr. Prince's suit from Mom:

I may have to move it soon, though. It's really starting to stink!

Then I spent the whole bus ride making up a new clue to catch the Mac and Cheese Bandit.

It took me a hundred sheets of paper, but it was worth it because I discovered a secret formula!

Check this out:

That means Jack really is the bandit!

As soon as I got to lunch, I showed Dante.

Obviously Dante knows nothing about being a real private eye. So I went over to hang my clue next to my poster. Except guess what I found?

Someone had written all over it!

Plus, there was a big blob of
bubble gum stuck to the bottom!

I had to make sure no one saw it! Luckily, I knew exactly what to say.

But I was too late! They looked.

One thing I've learned: it's hard being a private eye at this school. Not everyone takes my job as seriously as I do.

Once they were gone,
I took the poster down
and tried to hide it in my
backpack.

But thanks to the gum,
it was almost impossible.
The harder I tried,
the stickier it got.

All I can say is
it's a good thing I know
how to deal with problems like gum.

After lunch, Mr. Toots came into our classroom to fix the leaky ceiling.

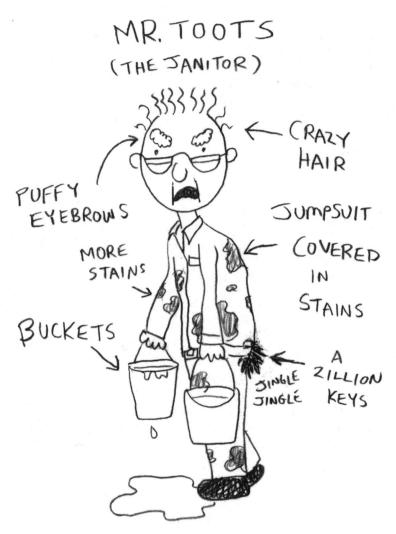

Even though he's the janitor, he acts like he's the boss of the whole school.

He's always yelling at kids not to touch stuff
that they would never want to touch in the first
place.

Like one time, when Taylor Schmidt threw up in
front of the art room, Mr. Toots stood right next
to the puddle, saying "Don't touch it! Don't touch
it!" to every kid who walked by.

I sometimes wonder if he's even a real janitor.
Because he didn't really fix our leaks.

All he did was leave some buckets around to catch the drips. He put one so close to my foot that I accidentally touched it.

I tried to put the bucket back where it was, but it was impossible to get it in the exact same spot.

It's too bad Mr. Toots didn't see the puddle . . .

. . . but it's a good thing the bucket was there to break his fall.

Actually, he should be happy I moved it. As you can see, I pretty much saved his life.

I think he was kind of mad about it, though. Probably because he had to go to the nurse with a bucket stuck to his butt.

Since that was his last bucket, Mrs. Sikes used the trash can to catch the drips. Thanks to her, I was stuck listening to the sound of dripping water all day.

TAP!
TAP!
TAP!
TAP!

Plus, you know how I always say that sound makes me have to . . . um . . . kind of . . . you know . . . PEE?

Well, I guess I'm not the only one.

Mrs. Sikes only lets one kid go at a time, so I had to keep my hand up for almost three hours. That's pretty much FOREVER when you have to pee as bad as I did!

So I made sure EVERYONE knew I had an emergency situation.

After that, Mrs. Sikes was glad to let me go.

And I made it just in time!

On my way back from the bathroom, I found another clue. It was a tiny piece of macaroni on the floor by the drinking fountain.

And guess who was standing right next to it?

As you know, an important part of being a private eye is avoiding traps. And this definitely seemed like a trap.

As you know, another important part of being a private eye is getting paid.

With my amazing eye for detail, you'd think I would have seen the gum that Jack had stuck to the fountain. Or at least smelled the barbecue flavor.

But it was too late. I got soaked.

When I got back to class, it was silent reading time again. I tried to sneak over to my desk without anyone noticing my wet pants, but I got the feeling that a few people saw me.

So I made sure they knew it wasn't what it looked like.

It was no use.

Pretty soon EVERYONE was laughing at me.

Everyone except Mrs. Silces. And I don't think she believed me either.

73

In the end, she sent me to the nurse to get dried off. But that wasn't the worst part:

On the bright side, I finally figured out how to clean Mr. Prince's suit with my ninja moves:

First, while Mom was upstairs putting Chloe to bed, I used my double-ended Ninja Staff to take the suit from its hiding place.

Then I used the
Shadow Warrior
pose to sneak down
to the basement.

There were already a bunch of towels in the washing machine. So luckily, I didn't have to figure out any of the controls myself.

I just did a *Dojo Dunk* and dumped the whole thing in.

Then I went back upstairs to play more **NINJA WARZ!**

About forty-five minutes later, I snuck back downstairs.

Success!

The mac and cheese was totally gone. Even the smell was a little better.

I was about to put the wet suit back into the bag when I spotted this tiny tag inside.

In case you're wondering, DRY CLEAN means it has to be very, very dry, or it won't be clean. So once again, my

amazing eye for detail pretty much saved my life.

I put the suit in the dryer
and pressed Super Dry.

Now I just have to stay
awake long enough to make sure
the suit is totally dry cleaned.

Then I can bring it back to Mr. Prince, and
Mom will never suspect a thing. Pretty sneaky,
huh?

Like I said, you can tell I'm already an
awesome private eye!

Love,

PJ

PS. Oh, no! I must have fallen asleep! It's midnight! I just ran downstairs to get the suit, and look what happened:

IT SHRUNK!

Now it looks like a suit for a baby! Or a big doll!

And it's all that tag's fault! It should have said WET CLEAN ONLY.

What am I going to do, Dad? Mr. Prince will never fit into this!

I'm doomed! DOOMED!

CHAPTER FIVE
THE UNDERWEAR LETTER

THURSDAY, APRIL 4

Dear Dad,

OK. I'm not doomed after all. Remember that piggy bank Grandpa gave me? The one that's shaped like a toilet?

Well, this morning I looked inside, and guess what I found:

nine dollars and sixty-three cents!

With all that money, I can BUY Mr. Prince a new suit!

It looks like all my problems are finally solved!

Just to be safe, I hid the tiny suit under my bed so Mom wouldn't find it.

Then I spent the entire bus ride figuring out how to capture the Mac and Cheese Bandit.

You'd be proud of me. I came up with the
perfect 3-step plan!

I folded up the plan and put it in my backpack. That way, I'll have instant access in case I forget any of the steps.

Later, at lunch, I showed it to Dante. But for some reason, he didn't seem too excited about it.

Meanwhile, I saw a bunch of kindergartners hanging up some posters for the Spring Fling.

The Spring Fling is this really horrible play that they do every year. Mr. Pastrami helps them a little, but you can tell they do most of the work themselves.

How bad is it? Just take a look at their posters:

Pretty bad, huh? That's because they only spent like thirty seconds making them. If you ask me, my posters are way better.

One thing I've learned: hanging posters at this school can be dangerous. So it was my job to warn them.

After that, they started running around screaming their heads off. I don't blame them for being scared of the bandit. But Mrs. Sikes got mad.

She made me spend the rest of lunch at the quiet table with her. Can you believe it? She didn't even thank me for my warning. Maybe she doesn't care about stopping the bandit, but I do.

Speaking of trouble, I have great news! Mr. Pastrami kicked Jack B. out of the band today for giving Max Orobo a trombone wedgie!

In case you don't know, a trombone wedgie is when you tie a hook onto the slidy part of a trombone.

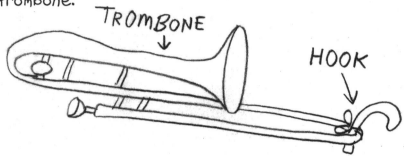

Then you catch the hook on the underwear of the guy in front of you . . .

. . . and pull the slidy part back!

It's the world's first musical wedgie.

Max's clarinet made this ear-piercing squeak right at the end of "I'm a Yankee Doodle Dandy." So Jack got caught red-handed.

As it turned out, Max was fine, but his clarinet needs fixing again.

Now that I think of it, his underwear probably does too.

After the wedgie, me and Dante were feeling kind of bad for Max. I wanted to help him, so I decided to write him this note:

If I was Max, I would have paid at least twice that much. But take a look at what he wrote on the back of my note:

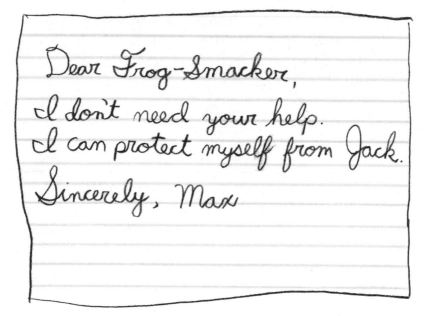

Dear Frog-Smacker,
I don't need your help.
I can protect myself from Jack.
Sincerely, Max

Can you believe it, Dad? How could he write that?

Everyone knows that Max is a way bigger frog-smacker than me!

All I can say is, while he's getting wedgies from Jack, the rest of the school will be safe, thanks to my 3-step plan.

In fact, during silent reading today I thought of one more step to add:

STEP 4: ROLL OVER THE BANDIT with a giant boulder.

OOPS

Awesome, huh?

That's sort of what my drawing looked like, but Mrs. Sikes took it away from me before I could finish it.

THIS IS QUIET READING, NOT QUIET DOODLING!

So I guess she also doesn't care about school safety like me.

Later, on the way home, I tried to redraw it. But when I took the plan out of my backpack, the bubble gum from my detective poster was stuck to everything.

Luckily, I was able to scrape most of it off on the seat in front of me before I got home.

I made it just in time! Mom was about to find Mr. Prince's tiny suit under my bed.

I decided to move the suit to the one place no one would dare to look: my underwear drawer!

I think it's safe to say Mom will never find it there.

Love,

PJ

PS. You'll never believe this, but Mom almost found the suit! Here's what happened:

After dinner, I was helping Chloe put one of your old ties on Teddy Snuffles when Mom walked by with a laundry basket full of MY underwear!

HE'LL NEVER ESCAPE NOW!

MOMMY! PJ'S TYING UP TEDDY!

I had to act fast! So in a panic, I said something I've never said before:

DO YOU WANT SOME HELP?

Then I sat down on my bed and started to fold my OWN underwear. You probably think I'm crazy, but it worked!

Mom got really quiet and sat down next to me. She looked like she was going to cry. Don't ask me why because I was really trying to help. Even to a private eye like me, the things that upset Mom are a mystery.

Anyway, I must have folded that underwear for at least twelve hours. Let me tell you, Dad, it was hard work! I folded and folded and folded!

After about six pairs, I started to sweat.

After eight pairs, I was completely EXHAUSTED!

I GUESS I'LL JUST FINISH THIS MYSELF.

Luckily, I had one tiny burst of ninja strength left to finish the job.

I don't think she figured out my trick. But just to be safe, I told her there was nothing I liked more than helping her fold laundry.

They must have been the towels that got washed with Mr. Prince's suit, because they smelled kind of bad. Even Mom noticed something weird about them.

I folded one towel. Just to keep her happy. After that, I was too tired to go on.

Mom told me I should go to bed. But when she went back downstairs, a miracle happened! My strength totally came back! It was just what I needed to get past the 5th-level dojo in NINJA WARZ!

Right now she's cutting up some fabric for Chloe's Spring Fling costume. She bought some new scissors today, and I'm not allowed to use them. So they must be really expensive.

That's fine with me. I'm too busy moving Mr. Prince's suit to a new hiding spot: at the bottom of Chloe's clothes hamper! I'm sure you'll agree it will be much safer there.

CHAPTER SIX
THE CLOSET LETTER

FRIDAY, APRIL 5

Dear Dad,

It's PJ. How are you? Did you karate chop any bad guys today?

I asked Mom if she knows anything about your SECRET MISSION. I hope that's OK.

She shook her head and said SECRET MISSION was a funny name for it.

What does she mean by THOSE GUYS? Are there a lot of private eyes in North Dakota? I thought it was supposed to be just me and you.

You'll be happy to know the suit is still safe! I checked again this morning while Chloe was brushing her teeth.

Then I got ready for school.

Today was picture day, so Mom forced me to dress up in a scratchy new shirt.

It was like torture!

Since I'm not allowed to use her new scissors, I couldn't even cut the tag off.

Today, at lunch, Mrs. Browny served creamed spinach. I dripped a tiny bit on my shirt, but it's OK. I don't think it will show up in my picture.

Besides, it's not my fault Mrs. Browny made it so drippy.

By now, the mac and cheese has been missing for four days. You can tell everyone really misses it.

So here's what I made:

Pretty awesome, huh? And it only took me thirty seconds to do it.

I'm not so sure about the reward part, though.
That was Dante's idea.

I made about five posters exactly the same.
But when I tried to hang them up, all the good
spots were already taken by the kindergartnel's.

There was
only one thing to
do . . .

Cover them up!

As usual, Mrs. Sikes had a problem with that.

I tried to remind her that someone WROTE on my last poster, but she wouldn't change her mind.

She said I was allowed to hang only ONE poster on the cafeteria door. Can you believe it, Dad? What good is ONE poster?

So I made her a deal:

Good thing it was easy to make new ones.

Plus, I thought of an even better place to hang them. A place where people like Mrs. Sikes aren't allowed to ruin stuff:

I had just hung up the last one, when guess who walked in. Here's a clue for you: he was chewing barbecue-flavored bubble gum.

Jack said if I wanted to hang stuff in HIS bathroom, I'd have to pay him fifty cents.

That's crazy! Everyone knows that the boys' bathroom doesn't really belong to Jack.

It belongs to Mr. Prince.

I almost used my 4-step plan on him right then. But he grabbed me before I could even do step 1.

Then he said something I didn't expect:

I tried to imagine what school would be like without Jack B. around.

He made a good point. That's a really BIG wedgie!

I felt stuck. It was a tough choice!

Suddenly, I knew what I had to do:

Pretty sneaky, huh? I think it's safe to say Jack didn't see that one coming!

And it worked too! In the end he let me hang all my posters up for only a quarter.

So this time, it looks like the joke is on HIM!

On the way back to the cafeteria, I found some mac and cheese right in front of Mr. Toots's closet.

It was another clue!

I ran back and told Dante about my discovery.

As you can see, Dante has a lot to learn about bravery. But I didn't have time to teach him. I had a mystery to solve.

This was a job for a real private eye. Someone much older and much wiser. Someone who laughs in the face of danger. Someone like me!

The closet was dark inside. And filled with buckets.

> I WONDER WHAT'S IN THOSE BUCKETS.

I reached for the light cord, but it was too high. So I got a bucket to stand on.

CLICK!

As I did, the door slammed shut.

I tried to open it, but it was locked! I was trapped!

Luckily, I spotted an air vent above the door.

There was no ladder, so I put
some buckets together to make
a staircase.

It would have been the perfect escape,
except one of the buckets was wobbly. I tried to
balance it, but everything went flying:

me, the
buckets,
and all the
black paint inside
them!

Luckily, I used
my *ninja* moves to
break my fall.

I pretty much saved my own life. Too bad I landed right in one of the paint buckets.

OH NO!

I was going to get in **BIG** trouble for this. There was black paint everywhere!

I tried to stand up, but I was stuck!

Then I heard footsteps outside! And I saw the doorknob turning! Was it Mr. Toots? Or Mr. Prince? Either way, I was doomed! The door creaked open. I closed my eyes and held my breath.

I have to admit I was pretty glad to see him. I didn't get in trouble, and I made it out just in time to get my picture taken!

As you can see, being a private eye here can be exhausting! So on the bus ride home, I rested my head and took a little nap.

Only, remember how yesterday I scraped all of that gum off onto the seat in front of me?

Well, it turned out I was sitting in the same seat!

I'm probably just imagining this, but when I got home, it seemed like Mom wasn't too happy to see me.

All I can say is, it's a good thing she bought those expensive new scissors.

Love,

PJ

PS. Bad news, Dad! After dinner, I snuck into Chloe's room to check on Mr. Prince's tiny suit. But it was gone! I looked everywhere!

If Mom finds that suit before I do, I'll be doomed!

On the bright side, at least I didn't get in trouble for messing up Chloe's room. When Mom saw the mess, she just told me to go to bed. I guess she didn't realize that it was still only 7:30.

She's lucky I'm here to keep track of stuff like that for her.

CHAPTER SEVEN
THE WEEKEND LETTER

SATURDAY, APRIL 6

Dear Dad,

   I couldn't sleep at all last night. It was horrible! Just ask Mom. I don't know how many times I woke her up to tell her. After the ninth or tenth time, she just said the same thing over and over again:

FOR CRYING OUT LOUD, PJ! READ A BOOK!

Maybe she thought reading would help, but it didn't. Mostly it just made me think about my own

mysteries, like the stolen mac and cheese and the missing suit. If I don't solve these cases soon, I may never sleep again.

When Mom finally woke me up for breakfast, I told her I couldn't go to school today because I had a headache.

For once in my life, it seemed like she actually believed me.

OK, PJ, WHY DON'T YOU SLEEP LATE TODAY. SLEEP VERY LATE!

Then, a minute later, I realized it was Saturday.

I guess Mom got confused again. If you ask me, she really needs to get her life organized.

Anyway, I'm glad I got up so early because it took me like five hours to clear the 9th-level dojo on NINJA WARZ!

I'd do a dance of joy, but Mom is taking a nap. So I'll quietly draw it here:

Let me tell you, Dad, NINJA WARZ is a miracle cure! Not only did I learn some incredible moves today, it totally fixed my headache too!

Although for some reason, it didn't fix Mom's.

She told me to do something quieter while she took a nap. So I decided to secretly search the house for Mr. Prince's missing suit.

Of course, Chloe bugged me the whole time.

There was no way I was going to tell HER about the suit.

So I made something up just to get her off my back.

It totally worked!

Sort of. Thanks to her screaming, Mom made me clean the whole house by myself.

Meanwhile, Chloe got to play dress up with Teddy Snuffles in her room. She didn't have to clean up anything. You call that fair? I don't.

On the bright side, I got your new postcard today! It was cool. But now I'm confused again.

Why did the SECRET MISSION move to Wisconsin? More trouble with bad guys?

You also talked about some guy named Johnny "DOC" Watson and his new ax. Is he a friend of yours? Why does he have an ax? Is that like a special ninja battle-ax? It sounds really dangerous! Where can I get a ninja battle-ax like Johnny "DOC" Watson's?

JOHNNY "DOC" WATSON

BATTLE SCARS

NINJA BATTLE-AX

HOOK

COOL PRIVATE EYE SUIT

By the way, I asked Mom if she thought the SECRET MISSION would ever move to this state. Good news! She said it is COMPLETELY up to you.

So what do you think? Can you move here? Please? Please? Please? Please? Please?

No pressure, but it would be way easier for me to teach you *ninja* moves in person.

Plus, you could introduce me to Dr. Watson. Just tell him to leave his ax in the car, OK? Mom says it sounds too dangerous to bring in the house.

More good news! She just woke up from her nap! Now I can finally do my dance of joy!

Love,

PJ

PS. I just did my dance of joy. Mom is taking another nap.

CHAPTER EIGHT
THE WEEKEND LETTER
(PART TWO)

Dear Dad,

Chloe was mad that I got a postcard from you yesterday and she didn't. I tried to pretend like it was no big deal. But she didn't believe me.

So I told her it's only because me and you are both private eyes and we have so much cool stuff in common, like doing ninja moves on bad guys.

But she didn't believe that either.

She only thinks that because she once found this really old picture of you in a disco suit from a bazillion years ago.

Just to prove it, I almost told her about the SECRET MISSION, but luckily I didn't. She's obviously still too young to know the truth.

Mom must have heard us because she forced me to help Chloe write you a letter. It took forever because I had to spell every single word for her.

At first here's what she wrote:

DEAR DADDY,
I LOVE YOU,
I LOVE MOMMY TO.
LOVE
CHLOE

But seriously, Dad. What kind of letter is that? It's like something a baby would write!

I told her a good letter has to be long and funny.

So I helped her spell a few extra words:

DEAR DADDY,
  I LOVE YOU.

  BUT PJ LOVES YOU
    MORE. HE IS
  COOL AND HAS
AWESOME NINJA SKILLS.
TEDDY SNUFFLES HAS
BARF BREATH. SO DO I.
      LOVE,
      CHLOE

Too bad she can't read it. I think you'll agree
it's **A LOT** funnier this way. Mom got mad and
crumpled it up. She said my sense of humor is
childish. No duh! What does she expect? I'm ten!

Thanks to Chloe, she made me spend the whole day grocery shopping with them. I think it was supposed to be a punishment, but I'm not allowed to stay home alone anyway. So it looks like the joke's on her!

Still, you know what I hate about going shopping with Chloe? We always see other kids from school just when she does something embarrassing. Like the time at Food Giant when she wanted to try a sample of spicy pepper noodles. Mom didn't feel like waiting in the huge line with her, so she made me do it.

MOMMY SAID YOU HAVE TO HOLD MY HAND!

TODAY'S SAMPLE: SPICY PEPPER NOODLES

I had to get out of there fast. So I secretly put extra pepper on Chloe's noodle. Just to make sure she wouldn't want more. What a mistake!

The next day at school, everyone was calling me Clueless Noodle Face. And it was all Chloe's fault!

Today, on the way back from Food Giant, we drove past a suit store called Tito's Big and Tall.

I asked Mom if we could stop and look around. Normally guys like me don't shop for suits, but I came up with an awesome excuse.

I WANT TO BUY A TIE FOR GRANDPA'S BIRTHDAY.

Grandpa's birthday isn't until next March, but I don't think Mom figured it out.

THAT'S VERY THOUGHTFUL OF YOU, PJ.

I thought it would be the perfect chance to buy a new suit for Mr. Prince. But it wasn't!

First of all, everything was really, REALLY expensive. There wasn't a single suit in the whole store for nine dollars and sixty-three cents.

Secondly, I forgot to bring my money. So Mom made me babysit Chloe while she paid for Grandpa's tie.

Just when it seemed like nothing embarrassing was going to happen, the door jingled and in walked Jack B.!

He was with some gigantic man! I think it was his dad, because they were both chewing gum.

Can you believe it? What was Jack doing in a suit store? I didn't want him to see me with Chloe. So I pretended to play hide-and-seek with her in a rack of suits. Of course, she ruined everything.

Then I remembered how something exactly like this happened to the private eye in Truly Creepy Crimes.

He had to hide from a gang of sinister janitors, but the girl he was with kept screaming.

So he saved them both by covering her mouth until the janitors were gone.

It would have worked for me too . . .

. . . except when I tried to cover Chloe's mouth, she bit me!

Thanks to her, I'm pretty sure everyone in the store heard us.

Then we got into a huge fight!

By the end, the store was a total mess! As usual, it was all Chloe's fault.

AS USUAL, Mom didn't believe me. So AS USUAL, I'm the one who got in trouble. Talk about embarrassing! Jack is totally going to make fun of me for this tomorrow.

During the car ride home, Mom told me to think about what I had done wrong at Tito's. So I did. And I'm pretty sure I figured out what it was:

I NEED TO GET BETTER AT HIDING!

When we got home, I found the perfect place to practice:

IN CHLOE'S HAMPER!

Plus, it was also a chance to spy on her and see if she knew anything about Mr. Prince's missing suit. Ever since Friday, Mom said I'm not allowed in Chloe's room. So I was taking a big risk.

What I saw wasn't worth it:

Finally, after ten minutes of baby talk, I couldn't take it anymore!

That was the loudest I've ever heard Chloe scream.

Mom didn't even care that I was trying to improve my hiding skills. She made me spend the rest of the day in my room with no NINJA WARZ!

Can you believe it? I didn't even find any clues.

Things can't really just disappear, can they?
Love,
PJ

PS. By the way, Chloe got your postcard after all. It was stuck inside a clothing catalog. Right next to a page with a bunch of suits.

It figures.

CHAPTER NINE
THE SCHOOL SAFETY LETTER

Dear Dad,

I didn't get any sleep again last night. And it's all Chloe's fault. She kept everyone awake with her screaming.

What a scaredy-cat!

Mom said if the noise bothers me, I should learn to sleep with my door closed.

So she was no help at all.

Not only that, at lunch today, I found my wanted poster stuck to the cafeteria door:

It looks like the bandit has struck again!

By now it was totally obvious that Jack did it!

As you can see, Dante still has a lot to learn about solving crimes. As usual, I had to handle it myself.

I spotted Jack outside at recess.

He was picking on Max.

I was about to use my 4-step plan to surprise him . . .

. . . but Mr. Prince ruined everything!

Thanks to him, I had to arrest Jack the old-fashioned way: face-to-face!

He wasn't going to fool me that easily! I know a clue when I see one!

Luckily, I quit.

After Jack left, Max came over. He was wearing a winter hat and one winter glove.

Don't ask me why, because it wasn't even that cold out.

Max is just a little weird like that.

What's important is the clue he handed me from his backpack.

It was one of Jack's old math tests!

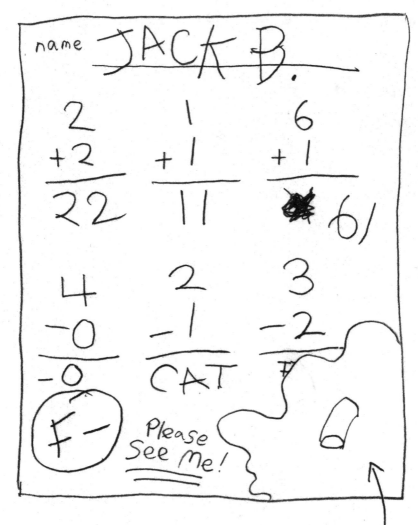

name JACK B.

$$2 + 2 = 22$$

$$1 + 1 = 11$$

$$6 + 1 = \cancel{} \; 6/$$

$$4 - 0 = -0$$

$$2 - 1 = CAT$$

$$3 - 2 = F$$

F-

Please
See me!

And look what was stuck to it: a piece of
macaroni and a little blob of dried-up cheese!

Now I had two perfect clues!

I told Max the only way to get Jack to show where he hid the rest of the mac and cheese was to catch him with my 4-step plan! Max agreed.

So we went over to the slide to start digging the spike pit.

There was only one problem:

Someone had left a soggy piece of bread lying in the dirt at the bottom of the slide. And neither of us wanted to touch it!

YUCK!

SEE IF YOU CAN MOVE IT WITH THIS.

I almost got it.

But then it went flying.

Fortunately, it just missed Mr. Prince.

Unfortunately, it hit Jack.

I had a feeling this wasn't going to help my case.

It was totally Max's fault for telling me to
pick it up in the first place. He took off running.
So did I. I ran as fast as I could . . .

. . . straight into Mr. Prince.

WHAM!

For once, I was actually glad to see him. It's just too bad he didn't seem glad to see me.

When we got there, I thought Mr. Prince was going call me a troublemaker again. But this time I got lucky.

ISN'T THERE ANY WAY I CAN TEACH YOU TO BE SAFE?

There was only one way I could think of:

FREE NINJA CLASSES?

Guess what! He didn't say no. In fact, he kind of liked it!

THAT'S A PRETTY GOOD IDEA, PJ. I CAN START A TAE KWON DO CLASS.

BUT WHO WOULD TEACH IT?

ME!

Can you believe it, Dad? Mr. Prince knows Tae Kwon Do! How awesome is that!

By the way, Tae Kwon Do really just means "karate" in a foreign language. So it's still all about doing crazy flips and chopping bad guys and stuff.

I started to think Mr. Prince might be the coolest principal on the planet. But that didn't last long.

He talked on and on about how Tae Kwon Do should only be used for peace and respect and stuff like that. It's hard to remember the exact words because I was busy thinking about chopping bad guys with the awesome new moves I would learn.

He must have talked for an hour!

By the time he let me leave, I was late for art. It's pretty much the only class I like. So I had to run through the halls as fast as I could.

On the way, I saw so many dangerous things, I lost count.

Just as I turned the corner by the band room, my foot slipped on a bunch of smooshed macaroni! I wiped out!

I'm glad I did, though. It meant I was finally on the right trail.

I was so happy, I did a dance of joy all the way to art class.

I got there just as Ms. Julian was handing out the cups of paint. It was perfect timing!

Well, almost perfect.

On the bright side, Ms. Julian has a poster on her wall that says "Happy Accidents." Now I finally know what it means.

Tonight, Mom helped Chloe do a drawing of her costume for the Spring Fling.

It turns out she's going to be a giant flower. This could be embarrassing.

Mr. Pastrami also told the kindergartners that they could bring their favorite stuffed animals to the play. So now Chloe wants to make a flower costume for Teddy Snuffles too. But Mom said she only has enough fabric for one outfit.

As you can see, Dad, Chloe can be a real baby when she doesn't get her way.

Well, I'm off to play some NINJA WARZ. But first I have to get my ninja suit. We both know I can't do my moves without it!

Love,

PJ

PS. Mom said my ninja suit is in the wash. Can you believe it? What am I supposed to do now?

CHAPTER TEN
THE SWEATSHIRT LETTER

TUESDAY, APRIL 9

Dear Dad,

It was freezing today. So Mom made me wear my sweatshirt from LAST FALL! By now it's like ten sizes too small for me! Plus, as soon as I got on the bus, the zipper broke. So I could barely even see.

I don't know why she doesn't just throw my old clothes in the trash. I could have been killed!

More bad news! I found out that the band will be in the Spring Fling tomorrow! And we sound TERRIBLE!

You could tell Mr. Pastrami was worried because he was sweating like crazy!

Plus, he made everyone play the same five notes of "Hot Cross Buns" more than a bazillion times! I only got to smash my cymbals once. But at least they kept me dry.

On the way out, he called me over to the side. I thought I was going to get in trouble for fooling around. But really he just wanted to fix my zipper for me.

I have to admit I never used to like Mr. Pastrami very much. But for some reason, he seems a lot cooler now. In fact, he may actually be the coolest teacher in the whole school!

I even wrote a hit single about him during silent reading. Mrs. Sikes took it away from me before I could finish it. But you can tell it's already the best song I've ever written.

I sprang into action!

I have to admit,
I was amazing!

Unfortunately, not everyone thought so.

Mrs. Sikes said my song was rude and disrespectful. So I asked her how many hit singles she had written in her life.

She made me finish silent reading in the hot spot. So I guess the answer is none.

On the bright side, I'll probably ask Mr. Pastrami if I can sing my hit single during the Spring Fling. I think he'd be honored, don't you?

During lunch, I saw Mr. Toots running around on the stage trying to catch drips in a bucket. Mr. Pastrami kept telling him where to go, but he missed them all.

It was kind of fun to watch. But you could tell Mr. Toots was getting really mad. When Mr. Pastrami tried to mop up the puddles, he ripped the mop away!

Then he turned around and slipped in one of the puddles. Suddenly, his legs started going crazy!

It was like he invented a brand-new dance! And he was awesome!

Until . . .

SPLASH!

. . . he got stuck in his own bucket again.

Mr. Pastrami had to carry him offstage like that. Meanwhile, everyone in the cafeteria burst into applause! What a show! If only the Spring Fling was that funny. Seriously, Dad. I would love to get that kind of applause someday. Wouldn't you?

After the show, I felt pretty excited about everything. Especially the mystery!

So I told Dante about all the new clues I found yesterday.

First the mac and cheese on Jack's math test:

Then the mac and cheese outside the band room:

As you know, I usually work alone. But Dante needed to learn about bravery, and I needed someone to watch my back. So I let him follow me.

The band room was dark. No one was there. It was safe to snoop around.

First we checked out the piano for clues.

We also tested out the drums and cymbals just to be safe.

Then we went over to where Mr. Pastrami keeps the brass instruments. And guess what we found?

I tried to follow it, but the trail stopped at Mr. Pastrami's tuba.

Then Dante found a big metal pan stuck inside one of the empty trombone cubbies.

I decided to take a look. But it wouldn't come out! Something was sticking to the pan.

I gave it one more yank.

Then . . .

It was almost empty. There was only a tiny bit of mac and cheese left inside.

But on the corner was a big blob of bubble gum!

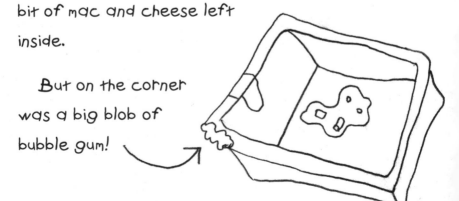

There was only one way to find out.

Then, thanks to my incredible eye for detail, I spotted another clue!

It was covered in mac and cheese! Dante was confused, but not me!

As you can see, I pretty much solved the whole mystery myself! All I can say is it's a good thing we searched the band room.

Just then we heard the jingle of keys. I'd know that jingle anywhere!

Luckily, I knew exactly what to do:

Maybe it wasn't the bravest thing I've ever done, but in situations like this, it's every man for himself. I only hope Dante made it out of there alive!

When I got back to Mrs. Sikes's room, it was silent reading time again. I sat down and pretended to read, but the whole time I was really thinking about Mr. Toots.

Now that he saw me snooping around in the band room, will he come after me like the sinister janitors in Truly Creepy Crimes? Will he want revenge?

Somehow I had to get out of school without being seen. If only I had a disguise!

My sweatshirt!

When the bell rang, I put my sweatshirt on backward so the hood covered my face. Then I got in the bus line and walked very slowly.

I couldn't see a thing, but the whole time I could hear Mrs. Sikes yelling at some kid to stop fooling around and walk straight. I wish I could thank him, because he made my getaway easy.

Even though I made it home safe, I still can't stop thinking about Mr. Toots. What am I going to do, Dad? I can't hide forever.

Plus, the mac and cheese is still missing. The bandit is still on the loose. And I have no idea where Mr. Prince's tiny suit is.

Maybe I'm just a terrible private eye, after all.

I think Mom figured out something was bothering me because she asked if I was feeling OK. I just told her it was a guy thing. She doesn't understand the life of a private eye. At least not like you do.

Then, just to make things worse, Chloe started bugging me too.

Don't ask me why, but for once, Mom didn't take her side.

Then Chloe sneezed, and a
piece of spaghetti came out
of her nose.

So Mom had to pull the
rest out in the bathroom.

Leave it to Chloe to ruin a tender moment.
Love,
PJ

PS. You'll never believe it, but now my ninja suit
is missing too! What am I going to do? I'll never
solve these crimes without it! Plus, I have to wear
my old pajamas now. They're so small that when I
try to chew my sleeve, I end up chewing my hand!

This would be a good time for me to move to
Wisconsin and help you with the
SECRET MISSION. Don't you
think?

I promise I won't
disappoint you.

CHAPTER ELEVEN
THE SPRING FLING LETTER

WEDNESDAY, APRIL 10

Dear Dad,

I'm sorry to disappoint you, but I've decided not to move to Wisconsin after all. Mom found my ninja suit in the bottom of the washing machine!

So now that it's clean, I should probably stay and catch the bandit.

It's my destiny!

Today was the Spring Fling! With the bandit still on the loose, I had to be ready for a sneak attack! So I secretly wore my ninja suit under my clothes! It was the perfect disguise!

There was just one problem: Mom let Chloe wear her flower costume on the bus. So thanks to her, I stuck out like a sore thumb!

I couldn't even use my backward-sweatshirt disguise because *Teddy Snuffles* was already wearing the sweatshirt!

One thing I've learned: it's impossible to go undercover with your little sister around.

At about ten o'clock, they called all the 5th-grade band kids down to the cafeteria for the concert. I had to hide behind the curtain while Mr. Toots pushed the lunch tables to the back of the room.

Pretty soon everyone in grades 1 through 5 came in and sat cross-legged on the floor.

I kind of felt sorry for them. Picture a million kids crammed into one tiny room. Plus, it's like a billion degrees in there!

Meanwhile, the teachers had it easy. They got to stand around the sides and drink coffee and chat like they were on a cruise or something.

At first I was glad to be on the stage. But under the spotlights, it was hot up there too. Plus, with my ninja suit on, I was sweating like crazy!

Everyone was talking really loud, so Mrs. Sikes turned off the lights. Then Mr. Prince came on stage with his bullhorn. He was wearing a bright green suit and a tie with flowers on it. He looked cheesier than ever!

Someone made a rude noise.

I think it was Jack B., because Mrs. Sikes made him stand next to her for the rest of the concert.

Once everyone was quiet again, Mr. Prince started the show.

A few kids clapped. One or two at the most. Then the band started playing.

The drummers drummed.

The trumpeters trumpeted.

The fluters fluted.

As usual, I just stood there.

Next, three kindergartners wandered onstage dressed like flowers.

Then about twenty more flowers came out carrying their stuffed animals. When I saw Chloe, I almost screamed!

Teddy Snuffles wasn't wearing my sweatshirt anymore. He was wearing . . .

... Mr. Prince's tiny suit!

TINY
PANTS
TOO! →

I couldn't believe it! I had to get that suit before Mr. Prince saw it. But how? I needed a distraction.

Before I could act, Mr. Pastrami walked out onto the stage carrying his tuba.

WHO WANTS TO HEAR A TUBA SOLO?

No one clapped.

He put the tuba up to his lips, puffed out his cheeks and blew.

Silence!

He stopped, shook his tuba, and blew again. Something was stuck inside his tuba. Something that stopped the sound from coming out.

Meanwhile, Mr. Prince was now just inches from his own suit. I was going crazy with fear!

That's when my amazing eye for detail noticed the tiny yellow drips coming from the bottom of Mr. Pastrami's tuba.

Then I remembered the trail of mac and cheese in the band room. And where it stopped!

Suddenly, I knew what was in there!

Everyone stared at me like I was crazy. Everyone except for Mr. Pastrami. He was still trying to play! His cheeks were beet red, and his whole body shook.

There was only one thing to do:

Ninja Moves!

The Samurai Slide!

The Falcon Flip!

The Tiger Tackle!

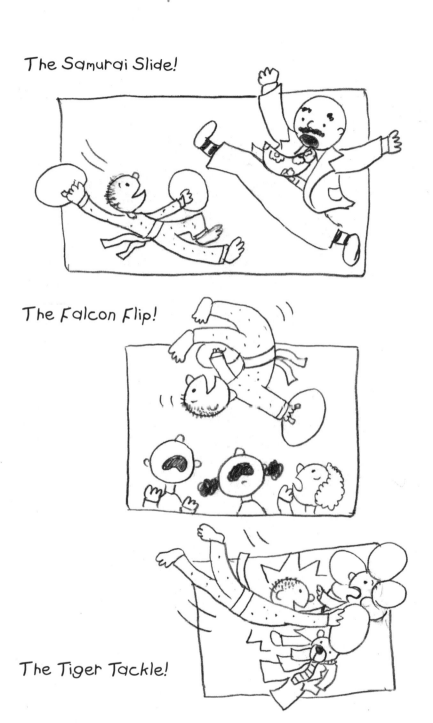

I pushed Chloe out of the way just as a gallon of wet, sticky, yellow mac and cheese blasted out of the tuba . . .

. . . and all over Mr. Prince.

HONK!!

But thanks to my ninja cymbals, me and Chloe
stayed totally dry!

It was amazing, Dad. I totally saved her life. I
was a hero!

PJ!
GO TO MY
OFFICE NOW!

Too bad not
everyone thought so.

BUT I
DIDN'T DO
IT!

As usual, Mr. Prince wouldn't believe me.

Just then a voice came from the clarinet section:

Everyone gasped.
Mrs. Sikes grabbed
Jack B.

Then another voice came from behind the curtain:

Everyone was shocked!

Then he tried to make everyone think that
Jack was the bandit:

He even took Jack's gum off of PJ's back and
stuck it to the mac and cheese pan.

The only problem was one of
his gloves got stuck too. That's
why he only had one at recess.

We put the wanted poster next to Jack's math test. Dante was right! The two signatures didn't match.

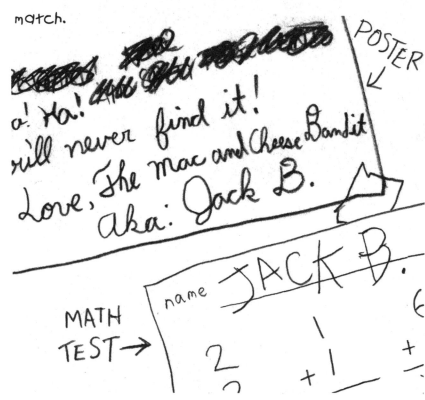

Then we put the poster next to Max's note.

It was the same handwriting!

Mr. Prince turned to Max.

Max was trapped! There was only one thing he could say:

Mr. Prince shook his head.

The crowd went wild. Everyone clapped and cheered like crazy! Let me tell you, Dad, getting all that applause felt good. Not only did I find the missing mac and cheese, but I caught the bandit too!

It was pretty much the greatest day of my life!

Afterward, Mr. Prince called me down to his office. Not to yell at me, but to apologize! He said he was sorry that he blamed me for putting the mac and cheese in Mr. Pastrami's tuba.

Somehow, I had the feeling that he was still mad at me for something.

I'm just glad he didn't see Teddy Snuffles wearing his tiny suit! Somehow I've got to get that away from Chloe before Mom finds it and starts asking questions.

Love,

PJ

CHAPTER TWELVE
THE HAPPY ENDING LETTER

THURSDAY, APRIL 11

Dear Dad,

You must be proud of me for saving the day yesterday with my amazing ninja skills. I mean, who isn't? But you know what's really amazing? Last night, Chloe didn't say a single word to Mom about what happened.

Of course, I also paid her nine dollars and sixty-three cents if she promised not to tell.

But it's still amazing, don't you think?

SIXTY-TWO... SIXTY-THREE...

Mrs. Browny served mac and cheese for lunch today.

EAT UP KIDDIES!

Everyone was happy!

Also, Mr. Prince is making Jack and Max eat lunch together until they learn to get along.
Good news! I think it's working.

Even I learned a valuable lesson from all this:

Just so you know, Dad, it does.

By the way, Dante asked if he could be my full-time private eye partner. I told him I'd think about it. He may not be very good at solving crimes, but he does have some useful skills.

Speaking of solving crimes, how's the SECRET MISSION going? Are you coming home soon?

I might do a project for the science fair, and I was hoping you could help me. I'm either going to make a fart-powered jet pack or a skateboard that turns into a monster truck! You know. Something to catch bad guys with.

On the bus ride home, I came up with the perfect 3-step plan to get Mr. Prince's suit before Mom could see it:

It would have worked too. But when I was going past Chloe's room to try it, I saw Teddy Snuffles just sitting on her bed, unguarded.

So I went in and grabbed the suit. I almost had it when—

So I tried to put the suit back on. Only Chloe wouldn't let me!

It was too late!
Mom caught me
red-handed. I was
holding the bear
AND the suit!

I thought I
was doomed!

But believe it or not, she didn't yell at me. She
never saw us fighting, so to her it just looked like
me and Chloe were playing dress up together.
Mom wasn't mad at all. In fact, she was really
happy!

IT'S **SO** WONDERFUL
THAT YOU'RE
FINALLY
GETTING ALONG!

How lucky is that! She didn't even ask where we got the suit from.

Then as a reward, Mom took both of us out for ice cream. Plan or no plan, I guess sometimes things just work out. Go figure!

Love,
PJ

PS. After ice cream, me and Chloe snuck up
to the attic to look for more clothes that Teddy
Snuffles could wear.

Chloe thinks we'll get more ice cream that way.

Well, we didn't find any TINY suits. But guess
what I found in your trunk?

It's your old disco suit from a bazillion years ago! It is shiny and awesome! Every time the light hits it, all the little jewels make rainbows.

DAD'S DISCO SUIT!

GIANT LAPELS

FRINGE

SPARKLING JEWELS

MORE FRINGE

MORE JEWELS

I can't believe you wore this! It may smell a little gross, but it's still the COOLEST suit ever!

Mom was going to throw it away, but I had a way better idea!

WAIT!!

Since I still owe Mr. Prince a new suit, I'm going to GIVE it to him tomorrow! FOR FREE! When he sees this, he is going to freak out!

Then all my problems will finally be solved! What do you think, Dad? I think it's the perfect plan, don't you?

Acknowledgments

Just like me, Jeff Mack
loves to write and
draw. He is the author and illustrator
of cool books like **Frog and Fly,
Hush Little Polar Bear** and
Good News Bad News. When he

was my age, he set booby traps for his brothers and
sisters and drew monster comics on his math homework.
He also got in trouble a lot, but I have no clue why. You
can visit him at www.jeffmack.com.

But enough about him. I want to thank these people
for helping me with MY book:

Jeff's editor, Mr. Green. He is smart and funny and
liked all of my letters from the beginning. Well, almost all
of them. It was his idea to cut out the bad ones.

Mr. Pfeffer, who is Jeff's literacy agent. He is really nice and knows EVERYTHING about publishing stuff. He's the one who said I should write this in the first place. Seriously! He MADE me do it!

Jeff's mom and dad, who are cool and awesome and talk to him on the phone about HIS books all the time. Unlike some parents I know. Hint! Hint!

Ms. Paluck, who is Jeff's best friend, but I think she sort of likes me too. Jeff is always bugging her to say good things about his stories, but she tells him the truth anyway. Go figure.

Oh, yeah. Jeff also told me to thank his old band teacher Mr. Pofahl for playing "Flight of the Bumblebee" on the trumpet every time he asked. Thanks, Mr. P.

I WANT YOUR BRAINS! DUH!

SINCE YOU GUYS ARE SO SMART, I'M GOING TO TAKE OUT YOUR BRAINS AND PUT THEM IN MY ROBOTS!

CHEW CHEW

PRETTY SOON I'LL HAVE A WHOLE ARMY OF KARATE-CHOPPING PUMPKIN-HEADED GENIUS PRIVATE EYE NINJA ROBOTS TO TAKE OVER THE WORLD WITH!

HA! HA! HA! HA!

A WHOLE ARMY? BUT THERE'S ONLY TWO OF US.

YOU'VE GOT TO START SOMEWHERE.

I'LL BE RIGHT BACK WITH MY BRAIN SCOOPER!

MEANWHILE...

LOOK! HE LEFT THE DOOR OPEN!

BUT WE'RE STILL TIED UP!

NOT FOR LONG! LET ME SEE YOUR HANDS!

CHEW CHEW

PJ CHEWED THE GUM OFF HIS DAD'S HANDS AND FEET.

THAT'S REALLY GROSS, PJ.

BUT IT WORKED, YOU'RE FREE!

234